OLD MEN SHALL DREAM DREAMS

PHIL EMMERT

First edition 2022

Published in the USA by *thewordverve inc.* (**www.thewordverve.com**)

eBook ISBN: 978-1-956856-06-4

Paperback ISBN:978-1-956856-07-1

Library of Congress Control Number: 2022907436

Old Men Shall Dream Dreams

A Book with Verve by *thewordverve inc.*

Cover Design by Robin Kraus
www.bookformatters.com
Interior and eBook formatting by thewordverve inc.
www.thewordverve.com

FOREWORD

The prophet Joel wrote:

> *28 And it shall come to pass afterward, that I will pour*
> *out my spirit upon all flesh; and your sons and your*
> *daughters shall prophesy, your old men shall dream*
> *dreams, your young men shall see visions:*

When a man reaches four score and more years, what little mind he has goes back to his childhood and to the mistakes and the victories in his life.

This story is not my story, yet parts of it are similar. Parts may be similar to you or to others you've known. Or perhaps it is not your story at all ... at least not *yet*.

~ Phil Emmert

CHAPTER 1

The old man slouched on the porch swing of his home in a quiet suburb. He cradled a Daisy BB gun across his lap. Squinting his eyes against the morning sun, he searched for his elusive foe.

His adversaries were the pesky squirrels that were constantly digging in his herb garden and eating most of the birdseed in the feeder. One or two had felt the sting from his trusty weapon and had become more than a little gun shy. The sound of the lever action sent them scurrying to the shelter of the tall oak tree shading the yard.

As the morning wore on and the sun warmed his aging bones, Lukas Mahoney nodded off with his chin falling against his chest. He had a boyish smile of contentment on his face as he began to dream ...

He was at once back in his childhood, in his hometown of Smallwood. The date of June 2, 1947 had been circled with a red crayon on the First National Bank calendar hanging on the kitchen wall.

It was the boy's tenth birthday. His mamma was standing at the kitchen sink dressed in her summer house dress and a worn apron, washing the supper dishes. His dad had just come back inside the house after his evening ritual of reading the paper and smoking his pipe on the front-porch rocker. He commented that it looked like it was going to be a hot summer. "That's usually what happens after such a cold, snowy winter," he added to no one in particular.

Luke was still a little hurt and miffed that he had not received what he really wanted for his birthday. But he knew better than to whine. In his heart, he knew his folks were probably doing the best they could.

His mother had tried to ease his disappointment by baking him a delicious chocolate cake—one made from scratch. It was four layers tall and had ten candles on it. He would be content with his well-intended gifts: a pair of skates and new long pants. Up until this year, he had always received short pants, which he hated. His mother just had a hard time letting him grow up.

Luke actually needed the skates, which clamped on the soles of his shoes. His old skates were worn out. These new ones would transport him around town most of the summer. When he wasn't skating, he mostly ran around barefoot. The family had learned to save on shoe leather during the war. It seemed to just carry over.

———

Without waking, the old man shifted in the swing and swatted unconsciously at a fly which had settled for a second on his cheek. The scene in his dream suddenly changed like the second act of a play ...

There quickly appeared another little guy in Lukas' dreams. It was a boy he had not thought of, even in his dreams, in many a year. He was the kid who had lived across the street and was the envy of the other neighborhood boys.

His name was Fredrick McBride, but everyone called him Red. He had flaming red hair that hung down across his eyes and freckles so thick across his nose that he actually looked like he had a deep tan on his face. His eyes were as blue as the Indiana sky on a crisp fall morning. He wore a felt cowboy hat and imitation leather chaps, even on hot summer days. He fancied himself to be some sort of Western hero.

It wasn't because of his looks or the way he dressed that Red was envied. It was that fancy Daisy Red Ryder BB gun he carried everywhere he went.

None of the other boys in the neighborhood could afford such a fine weapon. This was the poorer section of the middle- to upper-class town, the south side.

The war had ended, and most of the adult men on the 400 block of Elm Street were laborers. The women mostly stayed home managing the house and children. However, the one exception was Red's family. They had a maid who cooked and cleaned. Red's mother was a member of the country club, played bridge with other wealthy ladies, and was involved in various charities. She tended to look down her nose at other folks on Elm Street.

The McBride's had moved into the house across the street just one year ago. Red's dad was the new plant supervisor at Hoosier Furnace & Air. It was a local factory that made oil furnaces and a newfangled appliance called an "air conditioner" that would cool a whole room in the summer. *Or so they said.* These appliances were positioned in a window, replacing the old box fan or the rotating fans with which most people made a room bearable in the hot, humid Indiana summers. The only house in the neighborhood that had not just one of these air conditioners but two was Red's house.

The kids in the neighborhood cared nothing about the air conditioners or the McBride's maid. But they sure envied that Daisy Red Ryder BB gun.

Red carried that air rifle in one hand, and every once in a while, he would shift the weight, and one could hear those little copper balls roll from one end of it to the other—obviously loaded and ready to go. Sometimes he would pull up, squint one of those cold blue eyes and shoot a telephone pole or the side of an outbuilding. The boys could hear the shot strike its mark, and Red would hoot, "I got um." He never said what he "got" exactly, but it must have been an imaginary bad guy holding up a stagecoach. All the other boys played that same game with pearl-handled cap pistols. Nothing came out of the end of those barrels except smoke that smelled like sulfur.

The neighborhood boys would harass Red and beg him to let them take a shot, but he just glared at them and shook his head. It was agonizing—they could just taste how delicious it would be to cock that lever action and shoot like the cowboys did in the Western movies over at the Lido Picture Show.

Sometimes Luke daydreamed about sneaking over to Red's house late at night, crawling in a window, and taking that gun. Going up to a streetlight and shooting it till the BBs were gone. But he suspected Red probably slept with it. The only time anyone ever saw him without it was on Sunday morning when he headed to the large, uptown Methodist church with his mom and dad.

When Christmas rolled around, Luke more than hinted that he *really needed* a genuine Daisy Red Ryder air rifle. His mom just rolled her eyes at him, which meant, *That's not going to happen.* Just like when his daddy frowned—same meaning. Sure enough, on Christmas morning once again, Luke was disappointed. Mostly clothing—a new coat, leather shoes, a pair of rubber overshoes—and definitely no BB gun. His folks believed in practical gifts. They vividly remembered the days of the Great Depression. The hardships were still stuck in their mind. There was no guarantee that times would always be as good as they were now.

So all the rest of that winter and spring, Luke just followed Red around hoping he would tire of his weapon, lay it down, and forget what he had done with it. But alas, it never happened. Red loved that BB gun.

For almost two years, Luke window-shopped at Cox's Seed, Feed and Hardware. He wistfully coveted the beautiful black-barrel, walnut-stock Red Ryder air rifle resting in the gun rack behind the counter. His dream of owning such a fine weapon took almost sixty years to fulfill.

CHAPTER 2

The day of fulfillment came about one day when old
Lukas was browsing through Walmart, shopping for dog
food. The old man spied an air rifle hanging on the wall
behind the sporting goods counter. He could hardly
believe his eyes.

There it was, beckoning to him ... a shiny black barrel,
walnut stock, complete with a leather thong. Imprinted on
the stock were the words "Red Ryder." But he imagined he
could see *his* name written all over it. It was just like the
one Red McBride had owned so many years ago.

The signage next to it said that the handsome air rifle
could be his for only $31.99 plus tax.

Lukas' parents had been gone for years. He didn't have
to ask permission. He didn't have to wait for Christmas or
his birthday. Unlike in his childhood, Lukas always had
money in his pocket. Pulling out two twenty dollar bills
from his bulging, worn wallet, Lukas purchased the
dream of his boyhood. The old man forgot all about the

dog food as he walked out with that classic beauty in a box, along with a thousand copper shot. He was so elated he felt like he was ten years old again. Lukas smiled to himself as he thought, *Don't tell me money can't buy happiness.*

————

The old man didn't change up his routine much since he'd retired. He still arose between five and five thirty, just as he had done for the last fifty years. He had never required much sleep. Usually he slept no more than five or six hours a night. However, he did catnap some during the day, especially since his retirement.

Every morning, Lukas made a pot of coffee, which would last all day. And he ate his oatmeal just like the doctor ordered. His main activities consisted of puttering in his herb and rose garden, where he pulled weeds or trimmed up a plant. He also kept up with the lawn on his John Deere rider mower once a week. He could afford to have his vehicles serviced at the gas station, but he still did it himself. Even though he found it more difficult and slower to lie on that creeper to change the oil ... well, old habits were hard to break.

The old man often had interesting conversations with Molly, his loyal pit bull mix. She was never more than a few feet from his heels. He would ask her what she thought about the spacing between the plants or if she wanted another kind of treat. She would cock her head to one side and softly whimper an answer.

Sometimes he drove to the diner at the edge of town where he drank coffee, ate a cheese biscuit, told jokes, and reminisced with the other "old boys." Molly always took her position riding shotgun in his well-used F-150 and slept curled up in the cab until he returned. There was often a table where several older widow ladies sat looking at the old men while whispering and laughing amongst themselves.

Lukas always saved a morsel of cheese biscuit for Molly. She would take it in her mouth and carefully lay it on the seat, giving him a lick on the side of the face before devouring the treat. It was her way of thanking him for remembering her.

But after a time, the jokes got stale, the tales got more ridiculous, and the ladies got more flirtatious. He would cease going to the diner for a while.

One rainy spring morning, after a trip to the diner for a cheese biscuit and the latest rumor, the old man sat on the porch swing listening to the raindrops nurture his herb garden. The soothing sound of water running off the roof made him drowsy. He drifted off into a very peaceful sleep and was back in his boyhood again ...

CHAPTER 3

The polished wood and metal telephone on the wall was ringing the family's familiar ring on the party line—two shorts and a long. The boy's mother answered as she always did, with her soft Midwestern "good mornin'." By the inflection in her voice, Luke could tell it was her sister Chris on the other end. After some small talk and a little gossip, he heard his mother say, "Yes, that would be fine. I'll have him all ready whenever he needs him." After a pause, she added, "Now you make him mind and don't spoil him."

Hanging up, she turned and saw the inquisitive look on Luke's face. She said, "Uncle Don wants you to help on the farm this summer." Now, Luke was elated at the chance, because he was pretty sure his uncle Don would let him drive his old green John Deere tractor with its distinctive *putt-putt-putt* sound.

He also knew there would be fishing in the gravel pit

for catfish and squirrel hunting with Don's single-shot .22 rifle in the woods across the road from the farm.

A few days later, on a June morning not long after his birthday, Uncle Don drove up in his *"like new"* shiny, black *"39"* Ford sedan. It was *like new* because all the while Don had been gone during the war, it had been covered up and on blocks in a barn, just waiting for his return. Don and Chris usually only drove it to town on Saturday afternoon when they grocery-shopped and socialized. They also drove it to church on Sunday and for special occasions, like picking up their favorite nephew. Throughout the week, Uncle Don drove his old 1933 Ford pickup with stock racks on the back.

Luke and his family never took long trips, so they didn't have a suitcase. His mother had put four changes of clothes in two large, brown-paper grocery bags. There were three sets of everyday clothes and one "Sunday" outfit. She sent Luke off to the farm with a warning to be good and do as he was told. But Luke was always on his best behavior when he was with Uncle Don.

Donald D. Gooden was his full name. He was a big, rough-talking man who always dressed in bib overalls, except on Sunday. He had a farmer's tan and often had an unlit cigar in his mouth, which he chewed and rolled from one side to the other.

Uncle Don had volunteered for the service right after the war broke out in 1941. He served in the Army Air Corps as a mechanic on B-17 bombers, and he sometimes went up in them for test flights. Don had been to so many strange countries, often speaking of his adventures in England, France, and Northern Africa.

He told about how so many people got seasick on the rough voyage over to England in a troop ship. He spun a tale of how they were rationed to one gallon of water a day while he was stationed in Africa. And that was why, according to him, he was prematurely bald—he never washed his hair the whole time he was in Africa. When Luke looked surprised at this, his uncle said, "Well, what would you do with only one gallon of water a day?" Then answering his own question, he said, "You would drink it."

Luke could sit for hours and listen to those stories. When Uncle Don finished one, Luke would beg him to tell another.

Uncle Don and Aunt Chris had no children, and Luke was kind of their adopted son for several summers until their own children—three girls—came along.

To a boy who lived in town, it was a delightful dream come true. They went to bed at 9:30 p.m. and rose at 4:30 a.m. Don taught his nephew how to milk the cows with a milking machine and to strip out the udder by hand. They milked eighteen cows and fed four sows along with about thirty half-grown pigs. Back into the house by 6:45, where a huge breakfast awaited the two hard-working farmers.

Sometimes before breakfast, Chris would ask Luke to feed the chickens and gather eggs. That wasn't too bad until he came to a nest with a setting hen on it ... and she would peck the fire out of him. When that happened,

Luke used one of the new words that he had learned from Uncle Don and knocked her off the nest. Then he would look around, hoping no one had heard him. Luke knew that if any of the adults had caught him saying those kinds of words, he'd have his mouth washed out with soap.

Aunt Chris would awaken and bake biscuits shortly after Don and Luke left the house. She fried up bacon or ham and a bunch of eggs. Once in a while, she would have a few pancakes waiting for each of them. Luke's folks never let him drink coffee, but Aunt Chris would set a steaming hot cup in front of him, just like he was a grownup. Luke poured in a great big dollop of thick cream that had just been brought in from the milk house and two heaping spoonfuls of sugar. Ever since the rationing of sugar had been lifted after the war, Luke couldn't get enough of it.

Even though Luke was small and wiry, he could eat more than most adults. Uncle Don would laugh and say, "I guess it makes him poor to pack it." Sometimes he would say, "Boy, you must have a hollow leg."

This meal would have to hold them until noon. No snacking in between meals except when Aunt Chris would sometimes wrap a leftover biscuit in a clean red bandana, wink at Luke, and slip it in his pocket on his way out the door. She knew a growing boy would need something more before dinner.

CHAPTER 4

If it was haying season, the neighbor men all got together and worked each other's hay fields, and the ladies brought food for the noon meal. It was a feast at midday, every day until the haying was all done.

The hay had to be mowed and then turned with a rake pulled behind a tractor so the sun would cure it. Sometimes Luke got to mow or rake, but he rarely seemed to do it to suit his uncle. After a few rounds, Uncle Don would hold up his hand and motion for Luke to get down. Then Don would take over.

One time, poor Luke really embarrassed himself. He was trying to show off for the cute neighbor girl named Carol. She was as pretty as a spotted pup, with long blond hair in pigtails. She dressed in short shorts and a blue denim shirt with the tail tied in a knot at her midriff.

Luke was paying more attention to her than where he was going and ran the sickle bar into a fence. After Don spouted off a few choice words and did some work with a pair of wire pliers, he freed the sickle bar and motioned for Carol to come to the tractor. She took over and handled that thing like she had been born on it.

Well, the truth was she practically had been born on a tractor. Thankfully, she never rubbed it in on Luke. She said, "Shucks, that could happen to anyone." But it had not happened to "anyone." It had happened to Luke, and his ego was pretty badly injured.

———

When the sun came out really hot after dinner, it was the time to bale the hay. Hay had to be pretty dry. Otherwise, when stacked in the barn loft, it could get dangerously hot, combust, and burn the barn down. There was usually at least one barn that burned down in the county during the haying season, when a farmer got impatient.

So, when the temperature rose into the nineties, that was when they started baling hay. That first summer, the baling machine was an ancient wire-tie baler. It was so old, the paint and lettering on it was faded, and one couldn't even tell the make, but it was likely an International Harvester. It belonged to one of the local farmers, but the whole neighborhood shared it.

One person drove the tractor pulling the bailer, and two people sat on the bailer itself, one on each side. One person pushed a wire into the bale, and it fed out on the other side where another person made sure the wire fed through a loop and tied the bale really tight. It was a hot, dusty, noisy job as the green clover or alfalfa was fed into the machine and was compressed into a tightly packed four-foot bale of hay.

Then, that eighty-pound bale was spat out on the ground. Next came another tractor with a wagon. One man walked alongside that tractor, picked up the bale, and deposited it on the wagon. The man on the wagon stacked the hay bales five high with a sixth row tying the bales together ... supposedly. If the ground was rough, sometimes a few bales would fall off.

It took six people to bale that hay, and the hay was still not yet in the barn.

The first year that Luke helped, the bales were just the same weight as he was, and he struggled to move them even slightly. It took Luke three years to grow enough to throw the bales on the wagon or to stack the bales.

When the load of hay got to the barn, the bales still had to go up into the hay loft. A large set of tongs that looked really wicked were used to accomplish this trick. The hooks were set into five bales of hay. Then a rope threaded through a set of pulleys ran to the back side of the barn and attached to another tractor.

When the signal was given, the tractor driver reversed, pulling the bales up and up and into the barn. At just the right moment, someone on the ground would pull the trip rope and dump the hay bales onto the loft floor. This procedure was repeated until the wagon was unloaded. Once in the barn, the bales of course needed to be stacked again. This procedure took another three people. The count was up to at least nine people to bale hay.

But wait—someone needed to carry water or iced tea to the laborers. This was where Carol and Luke came in. They kept the men refreshed and hydrated.

———

Usually it was the oldest man who pulled the trip rope and dumped the hay in the barn. It was physically one of the easiest jobs, but the timing had to be just right. An old neighbor named Frank was dumping the bales in the hay loft one day ...

Now, Frank was ancient, looking like ninety years old if he was a day. He was skinny as a rail in his oversized, faded bib overalls. His face had the appearance of leather from years in the sun and the elements. He wore an old, sweat-stained, felt hat and kept a chew of Red Man chewing tobacco about the size of his fist in his jaw. It seemed like he could go for half a day without spitting.

One day, Luke and cute Carol approached Frank with a large thermos of ice cold water and a gallon of iced tea. He was shuffling backward, pulling the trip rope so the forks would fall upon the bales in the wagon. There was a stock watering tank behind him with a board across it. Well, sir ... with one eye on the refreshments and the other on the forks, Frank backed into that watering tank, lost his balance, and fell backward, striking the back of his head on that board. Down into that watering tank he went

—completely baptizing old Frank. He came up sputtering and gagging. He gasped out in a wheezy voice, "I swallowed my 'baccer." All the while, Luke and Carol were trying unsuccessfully to keep from busting a gut while laughing. This was the closest Luke ever got to a whipping while staying with his aunt and uncle—a lesson learned in respecting one's elders.

———

Sometimes in the middle of the afternoon, a sudden thunderstorm would sweep in and put a stop to the haying for the day. Since it was after the noon meal, the crew was kind of full and lazy anyway. It was a wonderful time of fellowship. The men would gather on the porch and tell corny jokes and spin tall tales while drinking iced tea.

One such day, an especially violent thunderstorm was quickly approaching. Carol and Luke took shelter and were lying in the open door of the hayloft on some loose hay. All the while, they were looking out at the rain and trying to gauge the distance of the lightning by listening to how long it took to hear the peal of thunder. They would see a flash of lightning and begin counting. One thousand one, one thousand two ... and so forth until the thunder rumbled. It was supposedly one mile for each second.

As the storm raged overhead, Carol and Luke began to share dreams of what they were going to be one day. Carol planned to leave the farm, go to Hollywood, and become an actress, singer, and dancer like Betty Grable. Not Luke, though ... He was going to become the biggest farmer in the county, raising hogs. He already could visualize his farm and all his crops. He would farm hundreds of acres of corn, beans, and wheat. And as often happened to childhood dreams, neither was realized.

About as close as Carol got to her dream was singing lullabies to her four tow-headed children and dancing around the kitchen with her farmer husband while the radio blared country music. And Luke? He was as close to big-time farming right then as he would ever be.

CHAPTER 5

On Saturdays, farming ceased at noon. Everyone washed up and put on clean clothes. Aunt Chris would write her grocery list on a piece of paper cut from a brown paper bag. Although they raised most of their meat and vegetables, they still needed to purchase salt, sugar, syrup, coffee, tea, and the like. So they all loaded into the Ford and took off for town.

Not only was it a time to shop, it was a time to socialize. The men sat on the fenders of the cars parked around the square, exchanging stories, jokes, and bits of news. Much of the news was just gossip. Say what you will about the women; the men could do their share of gossiping.

The ladies and girls would walk around the square occasionally going into a five-and-dime store. Most of the time, they were only window-shopping until the harvest was in and they had some extra money.

The boys would walk on the low wall that surrounded

the courthouse. The concrete wall was about two foot high and ten inches wide. They pretended to be a thousand feet in the air, walking a tightrope. When they fell or were shoved off, they hollered all the way to the ground, just like in the movies.

Sometimes, as a special treat, Uncle Don would give Luke enough money to take in the Saturday matinee, buy a box of popcorn and a coke at the Lido Theater. There were always Westerns and short movies of the Three Stooges playing on Saturdays. A whole afternoon of entertainment cost about fifty to seventy-five cents.

When the streetlights began to come on and all the shopping was complete, Uncle Don and Aunt Chris went to Luke's parents' house. There they ate sandwiches and played a card game called Euchre until almost midnight, before loading up and going home.

———

Luke's folks didn't attend church much. But Don and Chris were faithful to attend a small church not far from their farm. So, dressed in their Sunday best, off to church they went each week, and Luke would join them. The older lady playing the piano was not very good, and the lady leading the singing was worse. The old preacher used words Luke didn't understand, and he often sounded and looked like he was angry about something. Different men were called on to pray, but Luke thought Uncle Don was the best. He used words Luke understood, and it was like he was casually talking to someone when he prayed. When Luke mentioned that one day, Uncle Don said, "Well, Luke my boy, I am talking to someone. Jesus is my best friend. He brought me back from the war." Luke remembered those words many years later when he finally committed his own life to Jesus.

CHAPTER 6

The old man sitting on the porch was startled awake by the sound of a loud trash truck out on the street. The Red Ryder BB gun was still on his lap. His faithful dog Molly was staring at him. He scratched her head, then reached in his shirt pocket and pulled out a treat, which made her jump to her feet, wag her tail wildly, and whimper. He tossed her the treat and she'd barely chewed it before it was gone. There were no squirrels in sight, so Lukas laid the gun on the deck and resettled himself back onto the swing. Picking up the morning paper, he decided he would read a little before the news grew too cold.

His eyes fell on the headlines below the fold:

National Guard Called to Help Evacuate Flood Victims

He read the story, which brought back a few memories, but he soon became sleepy. Dropping the paper onto the seat next to him, he felt his eyelids grow heavy, then close completely ...

The young man was dressed in uniform. Looking around the room, he saw other men, of all ages, dressed in Army fatigues from another era. Glancing at the mirror in his locker, a familiar face looked back at him. However, he had not seen this young man in almost fifty years.

It was as Lukas remembered himself in 1958. He was in the locker room of the National Guard Armory. The whistle of the first sergeant sounded, calling the men to fall in. There was a mad scramble for the door. All sixty-six men fell into perfect formation, at attention. The roll was called and each answered with a "yo," "here," or "present."

Sergeant Smith turned smartly on his heel, saluted, and barked to Captain Quick, "All present or accounted for, sir."

This was the 139th Field Artillery, Battery C, assembled and awaiting orders. Something was up.

There was a labor strike down in the southern part of the state. The dispute was so bitter that there had been some violence. This unit was being called out to assist in keeping the peace.

PFC Luke Mahoney and the others were ordered to draw their weapons from the armory along with several rounds of ammunition. Being a truck driver, Luke carried a .45 submachine gun, laughingly called a "grease gun," which was what it looked like. He secretly hoped he never had to fire it for real, because when practicing on the range, he couldn't hit the broad side of a barn with it. The gun was surplus from the Korean War and had fired so many rounds that the barrel was worn out.

Luke's ride was an Army-issue, two-and-a-half ton GMC 6X6, also known as a "deuce and a half." He drove while a gunnery sergeant rode shotgun; twelve men were in the back. They didn't take the artillery pieces this time, just personnel and small arms.

Arriving at the assigned destination, the men learned their quarters would be an old warehouse close by the factory where the strikes were happening, located in a little town called Jasper.

Almost everyone in that town worked in the disputed factory. Feelings were running high. Some wanted to settle, and some weren't happy with what was offered. The talks had ceased as no agreement could be reached. The strike had already lasted four months. Families were hurting. Some workers had tried to cross the picket line, and even outsiders—whom the union called SCABS— were crossing into town to work. It was nasty business.

The guardsmen, of course, could not take sides. They were ordered to keep peace and, if problems arose, to take in the troublemakers. The backside of the factory was fenced in, and a railroad track ran close by. No one was to cross the track or try to scale the fence.

One night, Luke was lying on his lumpy cot, trying unsuccessfully to sleep, when he heard yelling ... and shooting. Several shots echoed through the night air. The men could tell they'd come from different caliber weapons. A small caliber rang out, and then what had to be a large bore shotgun boomed. Almost immediately after that, they heard the report of two shots from a high-powered rifle. They knew from experience those two shots had to have come from a service rifle: an M-1 Garand.

Several of the men started for the door when Sergeant Smith suddenly loomed in the doorway and told everyone to stay put. Captain Quick and Sergeant Smith put Lieutenant Wall in charge of the makeshift barracks while they went to investigate.

Sirens could be heard getting closer. In about thirty minutes, Sergeant Smith returned, visibly shaken. Clearly, something serious had happened—a man carrying a Molotov cocktail had tried to scale the fence. One of the men on guard duty had spied him and called for him to halt. Instead, the interloper had pulled out a .32 revolver and fired at the guard. Then, from somewhere in the shadows, someone fired a shotgun at the guard.

The sentry had pulled down and fired on the man trying to climb the fence—two shots, both striking the man and killing him instantly. The revolver lying on the ground beside his body still had four live rounds in the cylinder. Whoever had fired the shotgun was long gone but a spent twelve-gauge shell was found forty yards away.

The driver's license in the dead man's billfold

indicated he was from Detroit, Michigan. A union-paid troublemaker from another state.

This news traveled fast, and when it hit the newspaper the next day, the negotiations immediately began again. Amazing how it took a tragedy to bring people back to the discussion table. Within two weeks, the strike was over and Battery C from the 139th Field Artillery Battalion was on its way back home.

On a sad note, the private who'd shot the fence climber never quite got over the fact that he had taken another man's life. Five years later, he took his own life by hanging himself in his garage.

CHAPTER 7

The old man awoke abruptly as Molly nudged his leg. She was ready for her lunch. He slowly pulled himself out of the swing and picked up his Red Ryder air rifle. He propped the gun behind the front door in its normal resting place.

In the kitchen, Lukas washed his hands, took a saucepan from the pantry, and opened a can of chicken noodle soup. He let it heat as he prepared a toasted cheese sandwich in an iron skillet. Reaching into the refrigerator, he retrieved an open can of dog food and put a spoonful in the feeding dish. Molly would just sit and stare at the food dish until the old man's soup and sandwich was ready. Lukas placed his soup and sandwich before him along with a glass of water. Then he bowed his head, blessed his food, and thanked God for all his blessings. Just the two of them would eat together—man and dog— with a silly one-sided conversation going on between them. Lukas would often pinch off some of his sandwich and toss it to Molly, who would catch it midair.

Next stop—the recliner. Memories came flooding back to the old man that afternoon as he settled into his recliner and Molly lay at his feet. He picked up the old annual from his high school, dated 1957, which he kept on the end table beside his chair. As he opened it, he thought of something someone once said: "The days and nights go by so slowly, while the years seem to fly."

He thought about how true that was. "The class of '57 had its dreams," just like the song said. However, dreams and reality are often worlds apart.

Thumbing through the old annual, there were hand-penciled dates beside some of the pictures with a notation: *deceased.* So many of his old friends were now gone. How he longed to recapture the days of his youth.

A page fell naturally open. Clearly, it had been a page oft opened. A beautiful young girl smiled back at him. Jean Hale.

Next to her picture was a handwritten note: *Jean Hale Mahoney, deceased December 5th 2012.*

There was an ache in the old man's chest, then tears formed and ran down his cheeks. His shoulders began to shake, and the sobs caused Molly to put her muzzle on the old man's knee.

Jean had been his wife for fifty-five years and his best friend for over sixty-five years. She had put up with his drinking for the first few years of their marriage. She had been so patient, loving, and caring while he wasted money on liquor and stupid purchases of vehicles and other things he didn't need.

She practically raised their two children alone. All the while, she prayed for him. She was faithful to her Lord, the church, and to her husband. He, on the other hand, had been surly and self-centered. Oh, how he longed for a second chance to start over with her and with the children.

Lukas first met Jean in the first grade at Stokes Elementary School. He had pulled her hair, and she in turn had smacked him. The teacher, Miss Ross, had only caught the last offense and scolded Jean. When Miss Ross turned her back, Luke smugly stuck out his tongue and crossed his eyes at the girl. She giggled at this while Miss Ross turned in their direction again, giving the girl an icy stare.

This was pretty much the way it went for the next twelve years. Jeanie, as he often called her, was "always getting into mischief," while the boy was sneaky and never seemed to get caught.

Luke never ever thought of Jeanie as anything but a best buddy until about the eighth grade. Then it was time for the eighth-grade dance. Before he could work up enough courage to ask her to the dance, she announced that Eddy Morris had invited her.

He was crushed. How could she accept the invitation from that greasy, slick- haired creep? And the fight was on.

For the next three years, Jeanie and Luke fought over almost everything. It all stemmed back to that eighth grade dance.

Then, in their junior year, things seemed to change. He planned far ahead of time to invite Jeanie to the junior prom, catching her just after the Christmas break. The prom had not even been planned yet, but he asked her and she accepted.

When he was with her, he felt complete. When they were apart, he just had a hard time coping. In their senior year, trouble was brewing. Luke found that he liked the taste of whiskey. He worked part-time at a gas station. When he got paid, he spent his money on booze. He had an older friend who would buy it for him. He often got so drunk that Jeanie would insist on driving when they were together. She likely saved his life many times by driving and covering for him.

Little did Jean realize that she was enabling him. All she knew was that she loved him. She wanted to rescue him but did not know how. So, after graduation, when he asked her to marry him, she said yes.

———

The wedding took place in Jean's parents' yard on July 10, 1958. It was a beautiful but simple ceremony consisting of only close friends and family. Luke and Jean agreed the money could be better spent on a nice house. A neighbor lady had baked a seven-layer cake for the reception, which also took place in the yard.

During their first two years of marriage, this happy couple rented an apartment and saved money by cooking at home. Their entertainment consisted of fishing in a gravel pit just outside of town and an occasional drive-in movie. Jean's parents had given them some old furniture to set up the house.

Luke and Jean agreed that she should continue to work at the local drugstore, where she had worked parttime behind the soda fountain while in high school. Luke pumped gas, changed oil, and did minor auto repairs in the daytime at a local gas station. And at night, he attended Clinton County Community College taking courses in mechanical art and specializing in diesel engine repair.

Just before Luke graduated, the owner of a little shop on the edge of town hired Lukas. The shop specialized in tractor- and truck-engine repair. It was hot, hard, and heavy work. But Lukas loved the challenges of repairing tractor engines and meeting deadlines so the farmers could get back in the field.

He came home tired and usually dirty. The first thing he did was guzzle down a beer and then another before supper. After supper, he showered and finished off the six-pack in the refrigerator before falling into the bed.

Jean was a good wife. She never nagged him that first year or so. Even when Luke started bringing home a pint of whiskey, she didn't say anything at first. But soon the pint became a fifth, which didn't seem to last too long.

He always was able to get out of bed in the morning and make it to the shop. It didn't seem to affect his work. But it did affect the relationship between him and Jean. She suffered in silence most of the time.

One day in June the second year they were married, Luke came home excited because he had found a house in the suburbs that was for sale and he could buy it on contract from the owner. He wanted Jean to look at it and give her approval if she liked it. The next day was Sunday and they went to look at the house. As they walked through it Jean was thrilled. She could make this house a home with just a little paint and minor repairs.

In December of that third year, Jean learned she was expecting. The baby was due in August. She became sick several times a week and was unable to cook or do the housework on those days. Lukas became irritable and verbally abusive. He never laid a hand on her, but his abusive talk hurt Jean more than anyone ever knew.

The hot summer days were the worst for both Luke and Jean. The house was often a mess, and she could only manage to make sandwiches for supper. It really didn't make a lot of difference to Luke. Usually his supper was beer, chips and a ham sandwich, with whiskey as an after-supper chaser.

The baby boy came, and they named him Mark. Lukas loved the boy, but he refused to change diapers, feed him, or give him his bath. To Lukas, that was woman's work.

Another fifteen months passed, and Jean bore a little girl. They named her Jenny. Jean cared for both children on her own; Lukas provided the basics, but not much more than that. He played with the children but felt clumsy when he helped put them to bed or tried to dress them.

Jean found she was pregnant again, but this time, something didn't seem right. She was even sicker than when she'd been while carrying Mark.

One Saturday night close to her due date, Jean was in a panic as she woke Lukas to take her to the hospital. After what seemed like an eternity, Dr. Jerry Elder came out of the delivery room with a sad look on his face. Taking hold of Luke's hand, he shook his head and said that Jean was fine, but the baby boy was stillborn. He told the nurse to take Lukas to Jean and then escort him to the lifeless body of his baby boy.

He was a perfect-looking baby and looked like he was only sleeping. He was perfect in every way except he had never taken a breath. The death of this little baby boy hit Lukas like a Mack truck.

While holding Jean's hand, he comforted her and gently kissed her several times. Lukas finally left the hospital, went home, and cried himself into a disturbed sleep. In the morning, he had no more tears left in him. His first act was to pour out an almost-full fifth of Jack Daniels and eleven bottles of Blue Ribbon beer. Right into the kitchen sink. He never touched another drop from that day on.

It is strange how a tragedy changes a person, and sometimes for the better. That was the case with Lukas. He vowed to become the best husband and father that he could be. And he kept that vow. He was about to make other changes as well.

CHAPTER 8

Lukas recalled a short passage of scripture he had read just a few days before by the prophet Joel. *Your young men shall see visions, and your old men shall dream dreams.* Lukas slept soundly most nights. But during the day when he napped, he nearly always dreamed very vivid dreams of years gone by. Sometimes, it was the late morning naps that produced such real visions of his past. At other times, it was his dreams after his lunch. But there always seemed to be a clear apparition.

One afternoon, Molly was especially attentive to Lukas. It was as if she was alerting him to something. She was never very far from him, but today was different. She stayed within arms' reach of the old man. He could not put his finger on it, thinking, *Too bad she can't talk.* Molly approached the table beside his recliner and gently placed her paw upon the high-school annual that was always there and whimpered softly. Lukas suddenly grasped what it was Molly was trying to tell him.

Today was his late wife's birthday.

Lukas petted the dog's head and said, "Thank you, old girl. You wanna go for a ride?" She pranced to the door, wagging her tail with the enthusiasm of a much younger dog. When Lukas opened the door, she beat him to the truck.

Lukas drove out of town past the Walmart, Family Dollar, and the Ace Hardware. Soon the town was in his rearview mirror, and the soft rolling hills on each side of him. About five miles out, he turned off the highway and found a small lane up a slight hill. The antenna on his truck made a twanging sound as it brushed the overhanging branches along what had become just a pathway. An eighth of a mile later, he turned through a gate with a sign that read *Edgewood Cemetery*. Even as isolated as the place was, it was a well-kept, older cemetery. Scattered randomly among the old markers were a few newer headstones.

Lukas parked under a spreading oak tree in the shade. He didn't get out right away. Molly looked at him and cocked her head, as if urging him to get moving. Lukas reached over and opened the passenger side door. Molly immediately jumped out and walked straight toward a familiar stone marker.

Two names were engraved on the stone, along with a heart, and in small letters was inscribed, *Soul Mates Forever*. This was the stone marking Lukas and Jean's burial plot. Off to one side almost hidden by a bush was a very small, well-worn stone with the name *Matthew*

Mahoney engraved on it, along with *Born & died December 15th 1963.*

Lukas recalled that he and Jean had chosen this site back when little Matthew had died. They had chosen their own headstone about five years before Jean had died.

Molly promptly walked around the larger stone while looking back toward the old F-150. Lukas was still behind the wheel, lost in images and thoughts of the heart. Molly trotted back to him and whimpered softly with her front paws on the driver's side door. After a minute or two, Lukas slowly exited the truck and shuffled to the grave. It was difficult for him, but he knelt down on his knees and bowed his head. He had a silent conversation with the only love of his life, and it lasted several minutes.

He told Jean how much he missed her and how much he still loved her. He smiled as he told her how Molly had reminded him it was her birthday. Her birthday was one of four or five times a year he visited her grave. He had no idea how Molly had known it was Jean's birthday. But he had found through the years that dogs have a sixth sense about these things.

Lukas told Jean he was sorry he had not stopped to buy some flowers or to even cut a few of his own roses. He knew she would understand. She had always said, "I want my flowers while I am still living." But a couple of times a year, he took flowers to her grave anyway.

After a while, Molly gave Lukas a wet kiss on the side of his face and lifted a paw. Lukas took the hint and rose to standing—with some difficulty as his joints popped and cracked. He made a mental note to bring a folding lawn chair next time he came. He also noted that the stone needed to be cleaned. He would take care of that next time as well.

Just before he turned toward the truck, he whispered toward the grassy mound in front of the stone, "I will see you soon."

———

Back inside the city limits, Lukas stopped at the Dairy Queen and bought two small cones, one for Molly and one for him. This was the way he and Jean used to celebrate her birthday. No sense in breaking with tradition.

Lukas slowly licked his own cone while holding Molly's cone for her to devour—which she did, in about sixty seconds. He smiled as he thought to himself, *I hope she doesn't get a brain freeze from eating it so fast.*

For suppertime that evening, Lukas set the table with two of his best china place settings and two candles, one at each end of the table. He prepared hamburger steak, gravy, mashed potatoes, and string beans. It was one of Jean's favorite meals. Lukas had cooked a small hamburger patty for Molly and put a dab of potatoes and gravy on top.

For a half hour, Lukas and Molly shared a nice conversation along with the meal. The talk was about "remember when" as so many past events were brought to the present once again.

He especially recalled how he had baked biscuits just one time in his life, when he and Jean were first married. The biscuits were so small they looked like they had been cut with a shot glass, and they were as hard as hockey pucks. As he told that story and laughed, Molly rolled her eyes at him as she lay with her head on her paws. She was full and just wanted to nap.

When the dishes were washed, he headed for the front porch with the old dog right at his heels. As he opened the door, they scared a couple of squirrels off of the bird feeder. Lukas settled on the swing and leaned back to enjoy the twilight. Molly did something she seldom did. She got on the swing with him and put her head on his lap as if to say, *This is nice*. It was the end of an almost perfect day. He hoped Jean had been looking down to enjoy it with them.

CHAPTER 9

As a boy, Luke had just tolerated going to church with his uncle and aunt.

As a young man, after his epiphany when he had that come-to-Jesus moment, he looked forward to sitting in church with Jean and the children. However, he shied away from anything more involved than simply going to church and sitting in a pew.

After the children left home, he and Jean remained faithful to Sunday morning worship. Jean attended a ladies' Bible study on Wednesday mornings. Lukas always said once a week was enough for him.

When Jean died, the church was very supportive and brought him food and uplifting words. So many different people called or visited him during that first week or so. After that, no one came by or called.

Finally, Lukas worked up the courage to go and sit by himself in the morning worship service at Old River Church of Christ once again. But it was not the same as when he was with Jean, holding her hand and listening to her beautiful soprano voice. Lukas found himself tearing up on several occasions and had to pretend he had a cold as he blew his nose and wiped his eyes.

One Sunday morning as Lukas sat listening to the music during the communion service, he sensed someone looking at him across the aisle. Glancing over, he saw an attractive older lady studying him. When she realized he had spied her, she quickly dropped her gaze into her open Bible.

All through the sermon that morning, the two of them exchanged glances. When the last *amen* was said and the closing chorus was sung, the lady approached Lukas and introduced herself as Lillian Marks. "But you can call me Lilly or just Lil," she added. "This is my first Sunday here, and I am sorry if I seemed to stare, but you look so familiar to me." Lukas introduced himself and told her that he understood, and a brief conversation ensued.

She had just moved back into Smallwood, and as a child, she had attended Sunday school and church at Old River. She said she had been away for fifty years. Her husband, who had been a career service man in the Air Force, had died about three months ago, and she'd decided to come back to the old home place, which was about three miles out of town. She was trying to restore it to look like it did when she was a child.

Since she was "new" in town, Lukas asked her if she would like to go to one of the local restaurants, Route 66, for lunch. Lil happily agreed.

Route 66 was a theme restaurant from the fifties. Lukas liked to go there once in a while and dream about the truly fantastic cars of that area. The walls of the restaurant were decorated with pictures of Chevrolets, Fords, Plymouths, Chrysler 300s, and souped-up model "A" Fords, as well as pictures of Elvis, James Dean, and the Beatles. The place always took him back to his teenage years.

Today, however, was different for Lukas. He and Lil chatted about their lives, capturing some highlights over the last sixty years or so. It had been a long time since Lukas had engaged in an intelligent conversation with a lady who wasn't the clerk at a grocery store or a bank teller.

Each of them seemed eager to share their histories and realized that forty-five minutes wasn't near enough time. They each paid their own lunch tab and left a tip. Exchanging telephone numbers, they promised to see each other in church the next Sunday.

CHAPTER 10

On Tuesday morning after eating breakfast at the diner and sharing a biscuit with Molly, Lukas found himself driving out past Lil's farmhouse. He remembered this place from his childhood. It had been a showplace in its day. He remembered his uncle Don talking about how all farmers should keep their places looking like that.

But the years had not been kind to the house or the outbuildings. They needed a coat or two of paint and some shingles nailed back on. Even the fences could use a friend as some of the posts were rotting away and holes had developed in the wire. Lukas found himself making mental notes about some of the repairs, even though it was none of his business.

———

After a light lunch of a bologna sandwich and potato chips, Lukas told himself it was time for a little nap on the porch. He fell asleep with his hand lightly touching the top of Molly's head as she lay at his feet. Just as he drifted off, Molly sighed, flopped onto her side, and allowed herself a nap too, dreaming about the days of her puppy-hood and chasing rabbits.

And Lukas dreamt of his boyhood yet again ...

Luke was once again riding in Uncle Don's old Ford truck with the unique growl from the exhaust of that flathead V-8. Luke rode with the window cranked down and the wind blowing in his face while his uncle pointed to the beautifully laid-out farmhouse and outbuildings of the McCormick place. "Every farmer should take as much pride in his farm," Uncle Don said as he rolled the stubby cigar from one side of his mouth to the other.

Luke thought to himself, *Uncle Don's place looks every bit as good as that, just on a smaller scale.* Luke didn't think anyone could do anything better than his uncle. And he often said so.

They were on their way to the sale barn to bid on some sows. Uncle Don had put the stock racks on the truck just in case they got a good deal. He could use four or five young sows.

Luke loved going to the sale barn. Several of the bidders had secret signals; and try as he might, he could not catch the signals. Some of these bidders were what the farmers called gyppers. They bought low and then found a buyer and sold high, making a profit.

Luke and his uncle walked through the pens and saw several young sows that Uncle Don made a mental note to bid on. He had a figure in mind that he would bid—and no higher.

As they sat in the bleachers surrounding the arena, the livestock was driven in, a pen at a time. The bidding began. The auctioneer rattled off numbers that Luke could barely understand. The man in the arena would look around and say *yes* from time to time, an indication someone had made a bid.

The auctioneer would occasionally make a joke that Luke didn't understand; but Luke would laugh right along with everyone else just as if he got the joke. Finally, the pen of five young sows came into the arena—the ones Don wanted to bid on.

Don didn't have a secret signal. He would just throw up his hand, and the auctioneer would recognize the bid. Uncle Don got the five sows for just under the figure he had in mind and was really proud of himself.

With the sows loaded in the back of the truck, the windows down, and the sows occasionally shifting in the bed, Luke was having the time of his life.

And then it got even better. Uncle Don pulled into a filling station and bought them both a bottle of coke out of a cooler filled with water and ice. Then they each bought a handful of peanuts out of a penny vending machine and put them in the coke. Luke was smiling from ear to ear and thinking, *Life just doesn't get any better than this.*

————

Lukas felt a tear at the corner of his eye when he awoke. How he longed to go back in time, if but for a moment, and tell his aunt and uncle how much he loved them.

Molly was soon nudging his hand for another pat on the head. She too had her own fond memories—of when she was a pup and able to run and fetch sticks. In these latter days, however, she was just satisfied to be in the presence of her beloved master.

CHAPTER 11

The next Sunday morning, Lukas was up early as usual. He found himself dressing for church without forethought. It didn't feel like such a chore, as it did all the Sundays before. He also found himself thinking of Lil. Should he sit next to her or sit across the aisle as he had done last week? He shrugged to himself; he'd figure it out when he got there.

The Sunday before, Lukas had driven his old truck to church. But this Sunday, he went to the garage and uncovered the beautiful, like-new Buick Le Saber, which had not been driven for several months. It was ten years old but only had fifteen thousand miles on it. It had always been "Jean's car." He had always been satisfied with his F-150. But he wanted to impress a certain lady today, so it was off to Old River Church of Christ in the Buick.

He tried to park as far from other cars as possible. He could not bear to get a scratch or dent by some careless car door. Inside the foyer, he spoke with several of the men about the weather and the prospect for the crops.

As he walked into the sanctuary, his eyes searched and found Lil sitting about where she had sat last week. It was decision time. He needed to make it quickly before folks became suspicious. Taking a bulletin from the door greeter, he made his choice. He sat about two feet from Lil on the same pew. She looked at him, smiled, spoke a soft greeting, and slid closer to him. She offered her hand which he took and shook—not too vigorously, he hoped. *There, the awkward part is over,* he thought with relief. Hopefully, she had not noticed his sweaty palms.

It was a nice service with good music and a special by a trio of teenagers. The preacher was in a jolly mood and put the congregation at ease with his good humor. The sermon was about helping others who were in need.

And with that, a light bulb went on in Lukas' head. Perhaps he now had a good reason to help Lil do some work on her home place.

After church that day, Lil invited Lukas to her house for lunch. She said it was not much, but it was more than she could eat at one meal. Lukas eagerly accepted the invitation.

At her house, Lukas set the table in the kitchen, a smaller table than in the rather large formal dining room. Lil served meatloaf, mashed potatoes, fresh garden peas, home-made biscuits, and iced tea. Then she brought out the tallest seven-layer chocolate cake he had ever seen.

It was obvious Lil had planned to invite Lukas for Sunday dinner. After dinner, she tied a flowery apron around him after he'd insisted on helping her with the dishes. She washed; he dried. And silently prided himself on not breaking anything.

All during the cleaning-up process, they talked about what all needed to be done around the farm in order to restore it.

Lukas asked Lil if she would like to go for a ride in the Buick. She smiled broadly and nodded. Luke thought to himself, *She sure has a pretty smile.* He opened the passenger door for her, and as he walked around the car, he wondered what Jean would think about this other woman riding in her car. He surmised she would be okay with it—she often said that all she ever wanted was for her Luke to be happy. And he was about as happy as he had been since Jean passed away.

Lil commented on how smoothly the Buick rode. Luke said, "They just don't make them like this anymore."

After riding around the county on roads he had not driven in years, it was time to return the lady to her home and call it a day. His Molly would be looking for her supper.

Lukas was not sure what to do when he said goodbye at Lil's front door. Lil made the decision for him. "This day has been a delight. Thank you," she said and surprised him with a light lingering peck on his cheek. It just seemed so natural that she should do this. She quickly turned and disappeared inside the house, and Lukas felt like he was walking on air all the way back to the car.

A perfect ending to a perfect day.

CHAPTER 12

When Lukas' phone rang at nine the next morning, he hoped it was not one of those irritating telephone sales people. He answered with a greeting that was more of a question than a statement: "Hello?"

He heard a soft Midwestern voice come over the line. "Good mornin'," and it sounded so much the way his mother used to answer the phone. He was in shock for a moment, but he finally managed to say, "Why, good morning, lady. How are you doing today?"

After a brief conversation about the weather, Lil asked him if he could go with her to the lumber yard. She wanted to pick out some siding boards for the barn and wanted to make sure she got the right material.

Lukas jumped at the opportunity. He offered to pick up the boards in his truck. But she said no to that—she just wanted him to help her make the right decisions; the lumber yard would deliver.

When Lukas arrived at the farm, he told her the first

thing they needed to do was to see how many boards she needed. He had his tape measure ready, and they walked around the barn, testing some of the boards. After counting which ones needed replacing, he measured and wrote the figures on a pad he kept in the truck. Then off to the Build Rite lumber yard in his old truck with Molly sitting upright between Lukas and Lil, looking first at one and then the other. Molly seemed just a little jealous of this strange woman in her master's truck.

With the order for the lumber placed, the three of them were almost back to the farm when Lukas had an inspiration. "Let's go to the Dairy Queen. My treat!"

He pulled into the parking lot and took everyone's order. He had a large dipped cone, Lil wanted fudge sundae with nuts, and of course, Molly wanted her small plain cone. Letting down the tailgate, Lukas let Molly jump into the bed and held her cone for her. She devoured it in about ten seconds. Back in the truck, Lukas and Lil didn't say much as they focused on their own treats.

This brought back pleasant memories for Lukas as he remembered the trips he and Jean used to take to the Dairy Queen. He couldn't explain it, but he had not felt like this in a long time.

Lukas dropped Lil off by the kitchen door at the side of the old farm house. "If you need anything, just call," he said, adding, "I'll see you Sunday." But he secretly hoped to see her before then.

After a light lunch consisting of a bacon-and-egg

sandwich and a glass of milk, the old man sat on his front porch swing, just thinking. He noticed a few leaves fluttering down from the nearest oak tree. For the last week or so, there had been a chill in the night air. Fall was just around the corner. He hoped that lumber Lil ordered would arrive there soon so he could get that barn buttoned up before winter set in.

———

That night Lukas had a dream. He was twelve years old and going into the sixth grade at Stokes Elementary School. He had new shoes, new brown corduroy pants, and a new checkered shirt. These clothes would have to last him until Christmas when he would get some updates. He had a new blue winter coat with a hood on it hanging in the closet. He could hardly wait until it got cold enough to wear. It had large black buttons and a belt to cinch it real tight around his waist.

Mrs. Patterson was his new teacher. She was a strict-looking lady with her gray hair pulled back in a tight bun. She always wore dark clothes, and he had never seen her smile.

She wrote her name in large cursive letters on the blackboard. Turning on her heel like a soldier, Luke almost expected her to click her heels and say, "Hiel Hitler!" The image made him smirk.

But he was brought back to reality as he realized she

was calling out names and different kids responding with, "Present, Mrs. Patterson."

"Lukas Mahoney," she said. Now, Luke had only ever heard his full first and last name called when he was in trouble with his mother about something. Luke swallowed hard and squeaked out, "Present" in a high-pitched almost feminine voice. He heard some giggles from behind him. Mrs. Patterson looked sternly over the top of her glasses for a moment, then went on to call out another name.

The pretty girl in pigtails sitting directly across the aisle from him was named Jean. They had been buddies since first grade. He didn't consider her a girl. She could climb a tree, throw a baseball, and skate almost as well as he did. She was always making faces behind the teacher's back. And when Luke laughed, *he* was the one who got in trouble.

All that school year, Luke and Jean were inseparable. She helped Luke with his English and spelling. He helped her with math. At recess and lunch, they were always together. They shared their lunches with each other. And when it was time for teams to be chosen, they always wanted to be on the same side.

One day, Jean fell while playing dodgeball, and Luke ran to her and sat on the ground beside her. He took out his hanky that he had only blown his nose in once, and he wiped the dirt off of her knee. She patted his hand and suddenly she didn't seem so much like a buddy. He felt different. He got red in the face as he thought about kissing her right on the mouth.

Springing to his feet, he ran to Mrs. Patterson who was sitting on a bench at the edge of the playground. He asked her if he could go to the restroom. She nodded in her firm way, and he quickly went and washed his face. He looked in the mirror. His face was still a little flushed, and he stayed in the restroom for a long time.

When he returned, it was almost time to go back into the classroom. Jean looked at him oddly and asked him if he was sick. Luke just shook his head and looked away.

For the rest of the school year, Luke had this mushy feeling inside when he first saw Jean each day.

Luke didn't know it then, but Jean had experienced those same feelings for Luke since the year before. They were now on the same page.

———

The morning after his most vivid dream, Lukas gazed at his aging image in the mirror as he shaved. *Luke, you are not a kid anymore,* he chided himself. He'd been battling some guilt feelings because he felt he was betraying Jean.

A few days later at the grocery store, Lukas was searching for a good steak at the meat counter when someone touched him on the shoulder and said, "Well, hi there, Lukas." It was John Addison, the preacher at Old River Church of Christ. They chatted a few minutes about the nice weather and how good the church attendance had been lately. Then something suddenly came over Lukas, and he blurted out, "Preacher, can I talk to you in private some time?" Looking a little surprised, John said, "Sure you can, Lukas. I'll be in my study this afternoon from one to five. Just come on in, if that's convenient for you."

At one thirty that afternoon, right after his lunch, Lukas knocked timidly on the study door at Old River Church.

Lukas confessed to Preacher John that he felt rather guilty about his feelings for Lil. John looked at him with a slight smile on his face. Reaching across the desk, he took Lukas' hand and said, "Lukas, your wife is not away on a trip. She is in Heaven and won't be back. No one expected you to jump in the grave with her. Jean loved you and wanted the best for you. Just because you have feelings for Lil does not make you an adulterer. I am sure Jean is smiling upon you right now. Remember what God said in Genesis 2:18. *It is not good for man to be alone.* And he made a helpmate for Adam. Put your mind at ease. Lil is a very good lady, just as Jean was a very good lady. My only advice is just go slow and think things through." Preacher John then had a short prayer with Lukas.

When Lukas got back in the truck, he felt a great burden had been lifted from his shoulders. He drove home thinking about what John had said to him. Funny how an intelligent conversation and a perspective from another angle could put one at ease.

CHAPTER 13

Leaving the Nest

After graduating from high school, Lukas and Jean's son Mark had gone off to Indiana University and was only home on weekends. He and Lukas had never been close. They often butted heads on trivial matters.

When Mark came home, he spent time with his mother or with his high school friends. Lukas was left feeling like Mark's banker, providing the money for his education—four years and then two more until he earned his medical doctorate. He was doing his internship at Methodist Hospital in Indianapolis. Mark was proud of his son but seldom told him so to his face.

One November day, Mark called Jean and told her he was bringing a friend with him for the family Thanksgiving gathering.

The day before the holiday, Mark drove up in his Mustang; in the passenger seat was a beautiful green-eyed girl with the brightest red hair Lukas had ever seen. This lovely lady's name was Marian. She and Mark both were interning at Methodist Hospital. Mark wanted to eventually specialize in heart surgery while Marian was specializing in pediatrics. They seemed a perfect match.

Jean and Lukas hit it off with Marian right away. There was much laughter the three days Mark was home. Just before they left, Mark said he had an announcement to make: "We are getting married in June."

After hugs all around, Lukas said, "Son, I know I seldom tell you this, but I ... we are so proud of you. And we could not be happier for you."

The following spring, Lukas and Jean traveled to Atlanta for the largest wedding Lukas had ever attended. Three hundred guests—mostly Marian's family and friends. Even the rehearsal dinner had been elaborate with steak, lobster, and wine. Mark had told Jean he felt out of place and was not looking forward to wearing that tuxedo, which he called "the monkey suit."

The wedding itself was beautiful. At the reception, there was a floating bar, from which Lukas abstained. The toasts were made, and the wedding cake was cut. A large dessert cart with sparklers on top was rolled out. The seven piece band played late into the night. It was indeed a joyful and memorable occasion. But Lukas was happy to get out of the monkey suit and back home to a more sedate life.

———

Their daughter Jenny was a whole different story. She had always been a quiet soul with a sweet disposition. She finished high school and then went to Indiana State for her teaching degree—her life dream was to help educate young children.

After graduation, she got a position teaching first grade, just like she'd wished for. The school was in Vincennes in the southern part of the state. It was there that she met Jerry McDaniel, who worked in the First National Bank in Vincennes. They had a small wedding in the Old River Church of Christ and a reception at Lukas and Jean's house.

Jerry was an ambitious young man and climbed the ladder to success quickly. Within five years, he was in charge of the loan department. He and Jenny built a new house and settled in. They were disappointed when they found they were unable to have children of their own. But Jenny took the children she taught under her wing, especially some of the poorer children. Eventually, Jerry and Jenny were able to adopt six-year-old twin girls from Vietnam.

Lukas and Jean loved the twins dearly. However, the family only got to visit at Christmas and for a few days in the summer.

Retirement did not come easy for Lukas. He had worked just about all his life. However, working on diesel engines was hard, heavy work. One day just before his sixty-fifth birthday, Lukas came home and announced a decision. He was going to the Social Security office the next day to begin the paperwork; he was retiring.

CHAPTER 14

But Lukas didn't get to the Social Security office the next day—at just before four in the morning, he was awakened from a deep sleep to the sound of Jean screaming. He bolted upright and saw she was holding her head. She said it was splitting with the most excruciating pain she had ever felt. Shaken, Lukas managed to get his wife into the vehicle so he could drive her to the emergency room.

By the time Lukas carried her through the doors of Methodist Central Hospital, she was unresponsive. In fact, she never spoke or opened her eyes again. She'd experienced a massive stroke in her brain, the doctor said, and was basically dead even before she arrived at the emergency room.

The next few days were a blur to Lukas. Mark and Marian rushed home, as did Jenny. Jean's family members were as supportive as one could ask. The arrangements were made and three days later, Lukas found himself staring at a mound of dirt in Edgewood Cemetery. He stayed until the grave was filled in and the flowers arranged around it. Mark, Marian, and Jenny and her family had to leave immediately after the services, but Lukas was grateful they'd been there. The sheer weight of having to think about funeral arrangements in addition to his sorrow would have been too much to bear without their help.

Back home, Molly was still walking around the house as if searching for Jean. She just didn't understand. On Saturday the next week, Lukas drove out to the cemetery in the pickup with Molly. She stood and sniffed at the mound of fresh dirt and lay down beside it. Lukas thought, *Now she understands*. From that day on Molly stuck closer than ever to Lukas.

A month later, Lukas was fully retired, spending his days tinkering with this or that, sitting on the porch, or preparing meals for him and Molly.

———

It is so true; most widowers do not seem to function as well by themselves. Lukas had convinced himself that he was fine with just him and Molly in that sprawling three-bedroom house. But there were times when he wished it was a might smaller. He loved his yard work, but each day seemed a little more difficult. The years of walking on concrete, tugging on heavy wrenches and laying on a creeper as he worked on trucks had taken its toll on his body. Then, just as he was thinking about moving to

Florida into a small retirement apartment ... that was when Lil came into his life.

Lil seemed to have given him new energy. She was only five years his junior, but she brought sparkle into any given moment. Almost daily they got together and planned the next step in restoring her farm to its former grandeur.

Lil had plenty of money for this project. She and her husband had made wise investments and other financial choices through the years. Whenever she suggested something for this project, Lukas would ask her if she had considered the cost. She just smiled and said, "You let me worry about the cost."

He later learned Lil was not just "comfortable" financially but was a multi-millionaire. He found this out accidentally through the local banker with whom he was friends. When Lukas learned this, it almost ruined their relationship.

Lukas began to treat her differently. After all, he didn't want her to think he was a gold digger.

One day when they were eating together, she looked across the table and asked, "Lukas, are you upset with me? You've been a little distant lately."

Lukas was silent for a couple of seconds. He didn't know what to say, but finally managed, "Lil, you are a very wealthy lady. What do you see in me? You could be having a grand old time down in Florida or in New York City with famous people."

Lil took off her glasses, stared long and hard at him in

a rather stern, school-marm fashion. Then just as suddenly, she broke into a smile and said, "Lukas, I am having a grand old time enjoying my life with you." Giggling, she added, "You old fart."

Lukas laughed as he had not belly-laughed in a long time. He had no idea she could even talk like that. They both laughed so hard that tears ran down their faces. Life was back to normal between them from that moment on.

CHAPTER 15

Winter came in the form of deep snow and extremely cold temperature; Nothing really new for central Indiana. On the second of January, Lukas was awakened at four thirty by Molly's cold nose on his cheek. He pushed her away but then realized something must be wrong. The house was cold.

He pulled the chain on the lamp by his bed—nothing happened. The electricity was off. Pulling on his pants and shirt, Lukas first checked the breakers, which were fine, and he surmised the problem was with the Rural Electric Membership Corporation. *Strange*, he thought. REMC was just about the best electric company around. Things like that didn't happen often.

Looking out the front window, he could not see much, but when he opened the door, he immediately realized the cause of the electricity being out. Ice.

A sudden ice storm hit overnight. Lukas found the flashlight he kept under his bed, then grabbed the oil lamp which was mostly used for decoration on a shelf. Lighting the lamp, he then built a fire in his fireplace. It had been a while since he had a fire in it. But the wood was dry, and it caught right away. Soon, the front room was warm. He quickly started the water faucets dripping. So far so good—no frozen pipes.

This storm had come on quickly and had not been predicted. He checked the thermometer on the post at the back porch. Lukas first thought that it must be broken. It registered a mere five degrees. And now snowflakes made an appearance. It was snowing hard at about a forty five degree angle. Lukas turned on his battery-powered radio and turned to an Indianapolis station. The cheery voice of the morning person said, "Welcome to January in Indiana." It was six degrees at the Indianapolis airport. The barometer and temperature were both falling, which was very unusual. The man on the radio said, "Folks, we're going to get at least eight inches of snow on top of this ice, and the temperature may drop to ten below tonight." Then the man laughed and said, "You're welcome."

Lukas turned the radio off. He'd had enough of that radio voice. Besides, he may need to save the battery.

Fortunately, the old F-150 was already in the garage next to the Buick.

At about eight o'clock, Lukas tried to call Lil. No answer. He figured the phone lines were down, just like the power lines. He ate a bowl of corn flakes and fed Molly. Leaving the empty bowl on the table, he put on his heavy coat, hat with the earflaps, and his gloves. Molly beat him to the door.

Lukas never worried about his truck starting. It started in any kind of weather. Backing out of the garage, he let it run at a fast idle while he closed the overhead door. He carefully maneuvered the truck on the treacherous roads. Not many people were out this morning. Schools closed ... and most of the stores too. Some gas stations and groceries with generators were open. He checked his gas gauge. Lukas was a cautious man; he always filled his tank when it reached half empty. The gauge showed the tank was almost full this morning. Onward he went.

Lukas reached Lil's farmhouse at nine o'clock that morning. There was a lamp light shining through the window in the kitchen. The door opened as he stepped onto the porch. Before he could take off his hat, he was embraced and given a soft kiss on the cheek. Lil was glad to see him. She'd heard the power was off all over Clinton County and most counties in central and northern Indiana.

While she talked, his focus was drawn to the smell of ... bacon? How in the world ...? Then he remembered Lil had a gas stove. She pulled out a chair and motioned to it as she turned back to resume cooking. Two eggs, four strips of bacon, two biscuits, and two cups of coffee later, both of them were chatting away and laughing like two kids. Lukas had not felt this comfortable with anyone since Jean had died.

Lil heated some water on the stove, and they shared in

the washing of the dishes. She also had a roaring fire going in the fireplace, which was one of those large, old fireplaces. It devoured a lot of wood but provided great heat for the living room.

Lukas went to the barnyard where a lot of old lumber had been strewn about, just waiting to be hauled off. He was thankful now that he had put that off until springtime. There were also some old logs in one of the fields that could be used if cut to proper size.

Lukas, Lil, and Molly loaded into the front seat of the truck, and they slowly drove back to Lukas' house—all the while, Lil admired Lukas' winter driving skills. Now, Lil had invited Lukas to stay at her house for the duration. He'd accepted the invitation, but he needed to take care of some things at his house first. No telling how long the electricity would be off. They noted many breaks in the power lines from the ice.

At Lukas' homestead, the fire was almost out in the fireplace. Only one thing to do, he turned all the water off, drained the pipes, flushed the commodes, and poured some antifreeze in the bowls. He went to the garage and retrieved everything he would need to cut the logs for the fireplace over at Lil's.

On the way back to her farmhouse, he stopped at one of the open stores to pick up any food they might need. Lil said she didn't need much as she always kept plenty on hand for such emergencies—something her late husband had always stressed. Maybe just some bread ... but of course, the store was flat out of bread. Luckily, Lil didn't mind making bread of her own. Wow, that brought back memories of his Aunt Chris. She always made bread when he was a kid. His mouth was watering at the thought of a fresh, homemade loaf of bread.

Back at the farm, Lukas drove close to the logs and cut fireplace-sized pieces. He and Lil loaded them into the bed of the truck. The snow was piling up by now and drifting. Lukas was glad to have the weight of the firewood in the bed of the truck as he drove. Back at the house, they carried most of the wood to the porch or into the living room.

By the time dusk rolled around, the bread was baked, and supper was on the card table in the living room by the fireplace. Besides the bread, Lil had also prepared pork chops, fried potatoes, and string beans. There had been great conversation all afternoon. When the meal was over and the dishes done, they started playing cards by lamplight. Neither had played Spades in quite a while, but it came back to them in no time.

As the evening wore on, Lukas became a little uncomfortable. Lil must have sensed it. She said, "Lukas, I'm going to fix you a nice pallet here on the floor next to the fireplace." She piled several blankets and a sleeping bag on the floor, then added, "And I'm going to sleep right here on the couch. Is that okay with you?"

Of course it was fine, and he said so. Molly was stretched out in front of the fireplace, no doubt thinking, *I have died and gone to dog heaven.*

Lukas banked the fire in the fireplace with a large log

just before he lay down for the night. When he folded into the sleeping bag, Molly snuggled right up close to him. And Lil called out softly from the couch, "Goodnight, sleep tight, don't let the bedbugs bite."

Lord, thought Lukas, *I haven't heard that since I was a boy.*

CHAPTER 16

Breakfast the next morning was just as good as supper had been. Cheese biscuits and scrambled eggs with country fried potatoes just like his mom used to make. Now Jean had been a good cook. But she'd never quite gotten the hang of fried potatoes.

All that day was spent feeding the fireplace, snacking, talking, playing cards, and reading. Lil had a great library of good books and magazines. Lukas found a stash of old *Popular Mechanics* and lost himself in the pages for two hours.

They switched on the radio to listen to the local news and weather at regular intervals. The snow had stopped, and the wind quit blowing, but the temperature was hovering at about zero. Snow plows went by every hour or so. The roads looked passable. The REMC folks were out working on the power lines. The voice on the radio said service would likely be restored sometime within the next twenty-four to thirty-six hours.

For thirty hours, Lukas and Lil played house. It was so much like being married except they stayed out of the bedroom and were careful to not get too playful. There would probably be talk and snickering at the diner anyway, being a small town and all.

The temperature rose, and the roads were cleared enough by Saturday that Lukas went back home and got his house in order. The plumbing still worked, and no damage was done.

On Sunday morning, Lukas got to church early enough to talk to John Addison in his study. He said, "Preacher, I need to talk to you again."

John gestured for him to take a seat. "If you don't take too long, I can listen right now."

Lukas shared about his goings-on during the snowstorm, told the whole thing just like it happened. Now, Preacher Addison was a really good listener. He kind of smiled, then with a laugh said, "Yes, I already heard this from one of our upstanding Christian ladies. But I know you and Lillian well enough that I didn't believe there was any *fornicating* going on." He put a special emphasis on *fornicating*, drawing the word out a bit. He then added, "Emergencies call for ingenuity. And it sounds like you and Lil coped very well in a difficult situation."

Lukas felt relieved and thanked John for his Christian attitude.

There were more snowstorms that winter, but the power stayed on. Lukas usually visited at Lil's for supper or for breakfast a couple of times a week. During these meals, plans for the farm's restoration were batted back and forth before being finalized on paper.

CHAPTER 17

The Indiana winter slowed the work on the farm. But by the last of June, the house and outbuildings had been painted. Lil tried to match the original colors as much as possible. The house and garage were sparkling white trimmed in dark gray. The barn and outbuildings were painted red, mixed special at Home Depot. There was not another barn around with that shade of red.

A crew had been hired to replace much of the fencing that had fallen into disrepair. At present there was no livestock, but in order to restore the farm, the fences needed to look like they had in the 1940s. There were no metal posts—they were all wooden. No electric fences either. As the old saying went, good fences had to be horse high, hog tight, and topped with two strands of barbed wire. And Lil had decided that was the way it would be.

As he approached Lil's farm one July day, Lukas had a flashback. He looked over at Molly and said, "Wow, old girl, this place looks just like it did the first time I saw it."

The scene before him brought back such wonderful memories. He was a boy again, hanging out the window of Uncle Don's old Ford pickup.

After pulling into the driveway, Lukas sat in his truck, taking in the view while stroking Molly's head. He sat there so long that Lil came out of the house and approached the truck.

"You all right?" she asked.

Lukas smiled at her. "Never been better."

———

Lil had been thinking about putting some animals on the farm. She felt like the restorations would truly be complete with the addition of some livestock.

When Lil approached Lukas with the idea, he agreed wholeheartedly. Adding a few farm animals would make the homestead complete and authentic. They began to plan. What kind of animals and how many?

Lukas reminded Lil that animals required a lot of care and could be expensive. She gave him that look again, the one that said *Money is no object here*.

Lukas suggested some sheep, a couple of calves, and some half-grown pigs. The chicken house was ready for occupancy, and the little pond behind the barn could use some ducks and geese. He also recommended adding just a few at a time and not all at once for a smooth transition all around. They then made plans to attend the next auction at the sale barn. Lukas was looking forward to it; he would get to show off his skill at bidding.

They drove to the sale barn in Lukas' truck, which sported brand new stock racks in the back. Once at the sale barn, they walked through the pens with the various animals. There were no sheep or calves that day, just sows with pigs and some boars. However, in one pen at the back there were two young goats. The man sorting the animals said they would not be auctioning off the goats today, but the owner was present. Maybe he would sell them right out of the pen. Motioning for the owner to come over, he then introduced him. The man told Lukas what he wanted for the pair of kids.

Lukas studied a minute and then offered him five dollars less.

Sold.

The young kids were as active and playful as anticipated. Once at the farm, they pretty much went wherever they wanted to go. And they were easy to care for. Within a week, they were considered pets, always underfoot whenever Lukas or Lil were in the barnyard.

Lukas purchased hay, straw, ground feed, and a salt block. Since it was summer, he only gave the kids a small scoop of feed daily and let them run free.

In the coming weeks, Lukas and Lil added four sheep, a sow which was about to furrow, and two calves that were just weaned. All ran together in the pasture. And all became so tame that they were almost a nuisance. But it sure was nice to see those animals in the barnyard and pasture.

One day Lillian heard a knock at the kitchen door and peeked out the window. A strange van was in the driveway. She answered the door to find a tall young man standing there with two excited youngsters next to him—a boy and a girl. The man said, "Sorry to bother you, ma'am, but we're on vacation from Chicago. We saw your animals in the barnyard. My children wanted to see them up close. Do you mind?"

The boy and girl bounced on their toes in anticipation. How could Lil refuse those sweet faces? She smiled and said she would be honored to show them her pets up close.

The man went on, "You sure have a nice farm here. It's the prettiest place we've seen." Then he motioned for his wife to get out of the van. Introductions were made all around, and then they headed for the barnyard.

They petted all of the animals and fed them bits of grass out of their hands. Even Sally the sow wanted her ears scratched. The little boy and girl didn't want to leave. Lil invited everyone to take a seat on the porch for some iced tea and homemade cookies.

Just before they were about to leave, Lukas and Molly drove up. The children petted and even kissed Molly on her muzzle. They said they couldn't have a dog where they lived. More stories and laughter were shared until the Chicago family reluctantly loaded back into their van, waving as they drove away.

Two more families from the city stopped by the farm that summer. They didn't come to the house. They parked in the driveway, reached through the fence, and petted the animals.

Lil took note of these visits from her kitchen window. Another idea was forming.

———

Lukas drove into Lil's driveway one morning in September. He and Lil had planned a picnic that afternoon at the back of the farm where a small creek ran through. Lukas had built a picnic table for such occasions and had placed it close by the creek.

After they spread the tablecloth and put the food on the table, they ate a leisurely lunch.

Lil said, "I've been thinking about something, a new idea I want to run by you."

"Shoot," Lukas replied.

"I would like to have a petting farm." He raised his eyebrows but didn't comment, so she continued. "So many kids have never seen a calf, let alone touch one. It is really sad. We got to enjoy these things when we were young. But these city kids don't. And I just feel they're missing out on so much. What do you think?"

Never one to commit too soon, Lukas said, "Let me think about it for a bit. I'll get back to you."

"Like, tomorrow?"

Lukas chuckled. "Give me a week or so. Want to weigh all the pros and cons."

And he did just that. A few days later, to Lil's delight, he agreed her idea was a good one. Setting up a petting farm would be a nice thing to do for city kids who had missed out on the fun of being a country child. But he added that she should check with her attorney about potential liabilities and exactly how to set it up.

Lukas also suggested that she consider the time involved in running a "dude ranch," as he called it. But by using that term, he unwittingly put another idea in her lovely head.

"You know, Lukas, this house is big enough to make it a bed-and-breakfast, along with a petting farm. What do you think?"

Lukas' response? "Let me think about this some more."

And he did just that. A few days later, Lukas told Lil, "Well, lady, it's your farm and your house. I'll support you in whatever you want to do."

Lil was clearly delighted, thinking about the children especially who would benefit from some exposure to country living.

By the spring of the following year, the petting farm/dude ranch/bed-and-breakfast was well on the way to becoming a reality.

Lukas organized the barnyard and the animals. He designed a pen of chickens and turkeys in one corner of the barnyard where scratch grain could be tossed to them.

He even built a chicken coop complete with nests so that fresh eggs could be gathered by visiting children. Lukas created a small pond for the ducks and geese in the pasture, just outside the barnyard.

One stall in the barn held two Jersey calves. An adjoining stall housed *a just fresh* cow, which visitors could milk if they came at the right time of day. There was a pony for short rides, and a pen of half-grown pigs. Every few weeks, these pigs would be sold and new ones would be purchased in their place.

There were several cats that had the run of the farm. Lukas smiled to himself as he remembered how his uncle Don had countless cats around his barn—and not a mouse or rat to be found.

After a final inspection of all the amenities, Lil was satisfied that her new venture was ready to be introduced to the public. She took out advertisements in *Country Living* and *Better Homes and Gardens* magazines for Lil's Bed & Breakfast.

That first summer and fall were slow. But starting in June of the next year, there were many guests at the B&B and a regular run of visitors at the petting farm. Somewhere about midsummer, Lukas came up with another idea: a hayride every Friday evening in the summer and fall.

Lukas found an old "A" John Deere for sale—and it was in pretty good shape—along with a trailer wagon with rubber tires that he was able to easily restore. And so every Friday evening, visitors came out for an old fashioned hayride around the fields on the farm, followed by a wienie and marshmallow roast around a campfire.

Sometimes someone would start a song and everyone joined in. Then much later in the evening, Lukas would tell a story from his boyhood—or, on occasion, a scary story.

Lil's Bed & Breakfast was popular with newlyweds and seniors, and the Dude Ranch was quite a hit with not just the children but with older folks who, like Lukas, experienced a rekindling of precious memories. Three years later, the project that started with just a tiny idea and some elbow grease was a thriving and in-demand business venture. Lukas had a reason to get up early each day, and it had also rejuvenated Lil. And Lukas began thinking he wanted more than just friendship from this relationship.

CHAPTER 18

One winter morning during the off season, Lukas had come over for breakfast and was on his second cup of coffee when he caught Lil around the waist as she cleared the table. She sat on his knee and giggled like a schoolgirl as Lukas whispered in her ear.

He had said it so low she had to ask, "What did you say?"

So he said it louder. "Lil, will you marry me?"

Lukas heard her breath catch ... and then she said what she had heard Lukas say so many times, "Let me think about it and get back to you."

Lukas smiled at her response. He owed her that much, in the least. He said, "Okay, gal, but remember I ain't gettin' any younger."

She lightly kissed him on the cheek and ruffled his hair. She knew he hated getting his hair messed up. They had a good laugh, but they both also knew the subject would come up again very soon.

The next morning, Lukas walked into the house with Molly on his heels, and the first words out of his mouth were, "Well, what's the verdict? You going to marry me, or do I have to start courting someone else?"

Lil took his face between her hands and kissed him hard on his lips. Then she let him go and said, "Yes, you old fart! I will marry you in a New York minute. And they both fell into a long embrace, so long that Molly eventually put her paw on Lukas' leg and whined. Seemed she was a little jealous, but she also wanted her breakfast.

———

The following Monday, Lukas and Molly made a trip to the Edgewood Cemetery. It was not Easter, Christmas, or Jean's birthday. Lukas just had something he wanted to talk to Jean about. He needed to tell her about Lil.

He remembered to bring a folding chair, an old towel, and a spray bottle of cleanser to spruce up the stone markers of Jean's and baby Matthew's graves. After cleaning the stones, he sat in the chair and began to pour his heart out.

He assured Jean that he had loved her more than anyone in this world and he had always been faithful to her, but he was lonely, especially at night.

"I have found another lady that I can love as completely as I loved you," he said. "Jean, you do understand, don't you?" And just as surely as he was sitting there, he felt a warm embrace around his shoulders, as if someone was hugging him. It was so real that he abruptly looked around. But he and Molly were alone. Grinning, he said, "I knew you would understand; you always did understand me."

The ride back home was different—more refreshing than it had been in a long, long time. Looking over at Molly, he noticed her eyes were closed, and he would have sworn she was smiling. He thought, *I don't care what anyone says ... Dogs can smile.*

CHAPTER 19

It wasn't long after their visit to the cemetery when Lukas noticed Molly had a little trouble getting up from where she was lying beside his recliner. Lukas examined her legs, and they seemed okay. When Lukas offered her a portion of canned dog food a couple of days later, she sniffed it, but that was all. At least she was drinking her water.

Lukas began to pay more attention to Molly. She was really getting gray on her muzzle and her head. He counted up from the year she was born and, to his amazement, realized she was sixteen years old! He couldn't believe it. Up until recently, she'd bounded around like a pup.

Lukas couldn't keep her water dish filled. She was constantly drinking water and then going out to urinate. She seemed uneasy, and her stomach was slightly bloated.

Unable to stand it any longer, Lukas took Molly to the

vet. The veterinarian was a new lady doctor in the county; *Dr. Susan Kemp* was printed on her sign. Dr. Susan examined Molly thoroughly and took blood, urine, and fecal samples. She wore a serious expression when she told Lukas to call her in the morning. "I should have all the results by then," she said.

Molly walked slowly to the truck then waited for Lukas to lift her onto the passenger seat. She seemed to be getting weaker by the hour. At home, she again refused to eat any dog food but did eat half a slice of bologna that Lukas offered her. She drank her water dish dry and went out to do her business.

Next morning, Lukas called Dr. Susan. The verdict was not good. She gave a very long name to the ailment. Lukas had never heard of it before. Dr. Susan said it usually only attacked very old dogs and most dogs didn't live long enough to die from it. She said, "Bring her in, and let's talk some more."

The drive to the clinic was the saddest day Lukas had experienced since Jean died. Lukas talked to Molly all the way. The old girl just lay on the seat beside him and only acknowledged what he was saying by slowly wagging her tail.

On the exam table, Dr. Susan stroked Molly's gray head and kissed her muzzle, then turned to face Lukas. "You do know what's best for her right now, don't you, Mr. Mahoney?"

Lukas swallowed hard and nodded.

Dr. Susan then stepped out of the room to give Lukas a

little time with Molly. Meanwhile, she would prepare the sodium pentobarbital for the injection.

In the five minutes Dr. Susan was gone, Lukas hugged Molly and told her it was going to be all right and that she would feel nothing. It was only him that would hurt for the rest of his days.

Dr. Susan came in, and Lukas felt a heavy weight in his heart. He held Molly's right foreleg as the needle went in, and in just a couple of seconds, Molly went limp in his arms and was gone.

Lukas took Molly home and buried in one of her favorite spots, in the shade of a sturdy oak tree out back. Her handmade wooden marker read: *Molly, gone too soon at age 16.*

CHAPTER 20

Rumors traveled at about the speed of light in a small community. The news that Lukas and Lil were going to be married traveled slightly slower, at the speed of sound. And everyone at church seemed to be so very happy for this couple.

Lukas didn't want their wedding to be a big blow-out like his son's wedding, and he broached the subject with Lil. To his relief, she felt the same way. Once the ladies of the church got involved, however, the guest list *and* the things-to-do list grew quickly. Lukas and Lil took it all in stride, thankful for the support and assistance. It took much of the pressure off of the happy couple.

The wedding took place on a Sunday afternoon in December. Two dozen people sat in chairs in the living room of Lil's farmhouse, which was decorated for Christmas in red and green with many candles. The Christmas tree shone from the bay window in the living room. Lukas shifted nervously from one foot to the other in front of the fireplace with his son Mark at his right elbow. John Addison, the preacher, stood in front of them. But all eyes were on a door that led from a bedroom.

At the appointed time, the door opened and a radiant Lil stepped through the doorway wearing a lovely blue dress and carrying a small white Bible in her gloved hand. John Addison's wife, Sarah, stood at her side as her maid of honor. Jack Houser, a member of the church, played on his guitar and sang the hymn, "Day by Day." The ceremony was moving but joyful.

That entire afternoon, people came and went during a floating reception, as refreshments were served in the large dining room by the ladies of the church.

There was no honeymoon trip, as Lukas and Lil had many things to do around the farm. But every day was a joyful experience together.

Lukas and Lil decide it would be best to move into Lukas' house. They had found that some of their B&B guests wanted to stay more than a day or two and wanted to cook meals for themselves in the well-stocked kitchen. Of course, if the guests didn't want to cook for themselves, Lil arose early and would serve them a nice country breakfast.

Lukas noticed that he did not nap and dream as he once did when he was all alone. His new helpmate had given him the energy, enthusiasm, and vision of a much younger man. In fact, Lukas' second marriage was more fulfilling than his first because he was a better husband this second time around.

Two and a half years later

Lukas bolted upright in bed and stared at the clock: 4 a.m. He felt anxious about something but had no idea why. He arose and tried not to disturb Lil. He kissed her lightly on the forehead, dressed in the dark, and made a pot of coffee—his usual routine. Lukas crept to the living room and almost fell into his recliner. He started to pray as he often did when he was by himself. He had only prayed a sentence or two when he felt nauseated and broke out in a cold sweat. He had a sudden pain in his chest. He found it difficult to breathe. Yet he finished his prayer ... "In the name of Jesus, amen."

About 6:30 that same morning, Lil suddenly awoke. She had a premonition that something was wrong. She did not often feel this way but had learned to trust her intuitions. She started to awaken Lukas, but his side of the bed was cold and empty. She quickly slipped out of bed and went looking for him. Lil found Lukas unresponsive, but still sitting upright in his recliner.

On the way to the hospital in the ambulance, Lukas was revived. He was rushed into the ER at about 7:30 and was admitted to the hospital.

The next afternoon, the family was present. Lukas realized his condition was serious. He had begged God to keep him alive until his family had all arrived. He wanted to see them one last time.

At four in the afternoon, Lukas closed his eyes and let

out a sigh. Lil, Mark, and Jenny stood together on one side of the bed, while Preacher John from Old Creek Church stood on the other side, praying an almost inaudible prayer.

A tunnel with a bright light on the opposite end opened before Lukas at the foot of the bed. A figure was walking toward him from the tunnel. It was a man dressed in a dazzling white suit with a deep-purple tie, and he was beckoning for Lukas to come to him.

Slowly, Lukas was lifted from the bed and then stood upright about a foot from the floor. He was floating toward the tunnel. As he stood beside the strange man in the white suit, Lukas glanced back at the bed and saw everyone looking down at the figure lying there. To his amazement, he realized it was himself—Lukas—still in the bed.

He felt warmth around his shoulders. It was the same kind of warmth he had felt that day years before in the cemetery as he spoke with Jean about Lil. He turned to see it was the man in white who had his arm around Lukas' shoulder. The man was smiling, and Lukas felt at ease.

He asked the man if he was a new doctor. "No, but I am going to take you to the one you have called *the great physician*."

CHAPTER 21

Lukas could feel that he was moving but he was not walking. He was now moving swiftly, faster than he had ever been able to run. He and the man in white seemed to be standing on a fast-moving walkway.

As they neared the end of the tunnel, Lukas heard music, and it became louder as they entered a most bright and colorful garden. There was lovely vegetation the likes of which he had never seen before. A charming brook flowed into a river; what looked like snow-topped, bluish-colored mountains could be seen in the distance. People sat along the banks of the water as if in quiet conversation. The music was still playing a tune Lukas had never heard before, but it was so beautiful he hoped it would never end.

Lukas asked the man in white, "Where is this place? Is this the campus of the hospital?"

The man chuckled softly and said, "Oh no, my son. This is Heaven."

At once, it was as if a curtain had been split in two from the top to the bottom, and off in the distance, Lukas could see two elevated thrones, upon which two figures sat. He could not make out any facial features of those on the thrones. Surrounding them were two dozen men dressed in white and many strange-looking winged creatures flying about.

Just about this time, the ones around the throne and the winged creatures began to sing a new song.

Holy, holy, holy.
Lord God almighty.
The great I Am who was and is.

You are worthy, O Lord, to receive glory and honor and power,
For you created all things and by your will they exist
and were created.

There was a dramatic pause ... then all the people who had been sitting by the waters as well as thousands upon thousands of other people, both men and women all dressed in white, of every race, began to gather as the music started again with everyone singing the rest of this new song.

You are worthy O Lamb of God; you are worthy O
Lamb of God.

For you were slain and have redeemed us to God by
Your blood.
Out of every tribe and tongue and people and nations
And have made us Kings and Priests to our God.

Worthy is the Lamb who was slain.
To receive power and riches and wisdom
and strength and honor and glory and
blessing and honor and glory and power
be to Him who sits on the throne and to the Lamb,
forever and ever.

The figure on the second throne stood, and his robe was so dazzling white that it was almost blinding. There was a glow around him, and Lukas somehow knew: *this is Jesus.*

Jesus was smiling, and he held up his hands as if to hush the crowd.

The people and the winged creatures that were around the thrones fell facedown on the ground and sang, "Amen and amen."

Lukas realized that he too was singing. But the language he and the others were using was not English. It was a new language he had never heard before. He also realized that his voice was exceptionally good. He had never before been able to carry a tune, but here, not only did he have a new language, he could actually sing on key.

There was absolute stillness as Jesus seated himself again on that second throne, and he began to speak. It was a wonderful story. It was a parable of welcome to all the newcomers to Heaven. And when Jesus finished, Lukas thought, *I wish he would never stop.*

The man in white told Lukas that he could now approach the thrones.

Lukas bowed down on his knees, and he heard Jesus say, "Welcome, Son. My Father and I welcome you into our Heaven." Jesus spoke with the most soothing voice Lukas had ever heard.

The man in the white suit laid his hand on Lukas' shoulder, and Lukas felt himself rising to his feet by some strange power, and he was able to walk effortlessly. He felt no floor under his feet. There was no gravitational pull; he was weightless. He realized he had felt no pain or discomfort since entering the tunnel. A sense of peace and well-being filled him, the likes of which he had never experienced in his lifetime.

Lukas turned to the man in white and asked, "Who are you, sir?"

"I am sorry I didn't introduce myself. My name is Michael, one of God's ministering spirits. And I have been sent to be your guide, temporarily of course."

Michael then beckoned Lukas to follow, and they were back on that moving walkway, but this time, they were traveling at warp speed. There was no sense of time lapse from the moment he had left the hospital bed.

CHAPTER 22

They were now at the entrance to a beautiful house. It was just like a house he had always dreamed of building. There was a doorway to the house but there was no door to open and close.

However, as he stepped through the entranceway into the house, he was at once surrounded by family members and some friends he recognized from his boyhood and from church who had passed years before. There was his mom, his Uncle Don and Aunt Chris. And then he spied Jean standing next to a young man who looked familiar, but Lukas couldn't place him.

Interestingly, they all seemed to be about the same age, somewhere around thirty to thirty-five years old.

Lukas asked Michael about that. "Is everyone the same age here? How can that be?"

Michael laughed an infectious belly laugh and said, "Yes, everyone here is thirty-three years old in earth years, just like Jesus was the last time he was on earth." He pointed. "You see that young man standing beside Jean? That is your son Matthew, and he is so happy that you are here."

The reunion was wonderful beyond words, and when Lukas was introduced to his son, it was as if they had never been apart. Jean had told Matthew all about his dad.

Jean hugged Lukas and said, "You're going to love it here. We sing, and we praise Jesus every day. We never have pain; we never feel hunger or thirst. You and I are not married, for we are like the angels who never marry. You see, we don't need helpmates here. But we are the best of friends like we were in grade school. It is better than a physical relationship ... I cannot explain it, but you will see."

Looking around, Lukas noted there was no artificial lighting in his home. No clocks, no calendars. No kitchen or bathroom. When he asked why that was, Jean laughed and said none of those things were needed anymore.

Lukas then asked about the winged creatures flying around. Jean laughed again and said, "Oh, Lukas, you will love them. They are so amusing. They fly around and sing, and when they are not singing, they are telling funny stories."

Lukas imagined they might be even more entertaining than TV had ever been.

He was standing next to Jean when he thought this, and Jean said, "Indeed they are much better than TV."

Lukas was shocked. *How does she know what I'm thinking?*

"There are no secrets here," Jean explained. "We all know what others are thinking. And since there is no sin here, there are no evil thoughts."

———

Jean, Matthew, and Lukas were sitting by the brook under the shade of the beautiful tree of life, when Michael came walking up with a lovely lady in tow. The woman had just arrived, according to Michael.

It was Lil, but she was much younger than the last time Lukas had seen her. There were greetings, sounds of joy and laughter, and hugs all around. Jean and Lil hit it off like long-lost sisters. Everyone sat and reminisced. And they would do this often. There was no darkness to indicate nighttime as on earth. They needed no sleep. They never got tired or sick.

Jesus would often come and tell them a wonderful story in the form of a parable. When they got to wondering about biblical questions that had bothered them on earth, Noah, Abraham, Moses, Peter, James, John, and Paul—and sometimes Jesus—would readily answer those questions.

Once, when Lukas was thinking how wonderful it was —eternity in Heaven—he realized there was one thing that would make it even better. *If only I could see Molly.*

Michael was standing close by, and Lukas heard that

infectious laugh as Michael said, "Lukas, come with me. I have something to show you."

They were again conveyed in an instant to a large area that looked like a huge park. There were all kinds of beautiful trees, flowers, ponds, and streams. Lukas noticed there were many animals in this park, and a few people were walking around—almost like in a zoo, except there were no bars, cages or barricades. There were animals that had been enemies on earth, predator and prey, living side by side. He saw cats, dogs, cows, horses, and even lions and lambs playing together. Lukas chuckled when a squirrel sat upright and barked at him almost like he remembered Lukas. It was the most amazing thing he had ever seen.

As Lukas walked around, taking all this in, he felt a nudge against his leg and heard a whimper. *What* ... He looked down, and there was a young Molly with her paw raised up to him. Lukas fell to his knees, hugged her and kissed her on top of her head.

"You can visit Molly any time you want to," Michael said. "This park is like every place in Heaven—it's always open."

Filled with deepening emotion and appreciation, Lukas nodded. *Yes, surely this is Paradise*

ABOUT THE AUTHOR

Born in 1937 during the Great Depression, Phil Emmert was raised near Lebanon, Indiana. At the age of thirty-three, he left a well-paying job with Dow Chemical Company, sold his little farm, and took his family to Knoxville, Tennessee, where he enrolled and completed four years at Johnson Bible College (Johnson University).

Phil preached in several small congregations in Tennessee and North Carolina. At the same time, he held several different secular jobs to supplement his income. As a school counselor, he wrote weekly inspirational thoughts for teachers and staff.

Phil also served in the Indiana National Guard for six years, 1956-1962.

At age seventy-seven, he published his first book, *When War Was Heck*, followed by *The Afterglow of War: Lessons Learned*, which were reflections from his childhood and teen years. Phil of late has changed his focus toward more Christian-based stories: *The Overcomers, America Rebooted, The Reprieve,* and this latest one, *Old Men Shall Dream Dreams.*

Phil acknowledges that he was a poor student in high school and even later in college. He often jokes that he wishes his teachers and professors could see him now. However, through his varied life experiences, he has become an appealing communicator and storyteller.

Phil and his wife Bea live in Washington, North Carolina. They drive fifty-five miles twice a week to a neighboring county where he still preaches in a small congregation.

———

Books by Phil

When War Was Heck
The Afterglow of War: Lessons Learned
The Overcomers
America Rebooted
The Reprieve
Old Men Shall Dream Dreams

Available wherever great books are sold, including the publisher www.thewordverve.com, in both eBook and paperback formats.